Disney
FROZEN II

JUMBO
COLORING &
ACTIVITY BOOK

bendon®

WORD UNSCRAMBLE

Unscramble the words below.

THIMCY

_____

DENDHI

_____

IIRTPSS

_____

ARNTEU

_____

BUILD-A-WORD

How many words can you make using the letters in:

WILDERNESS MAN

HINT:
*You can use letters
more than once!*

EXAMPLE: REINDEER

_____

_____

_____

_____

_____

_____

_____

_____

_____

_____

_____

_____

_____

_____

© Disney

SPOT THE DIFFERENCE

Find the 3 differences between the two pictures.

WHICH PATH?

Which path leads Elsa to the Water Nokk?

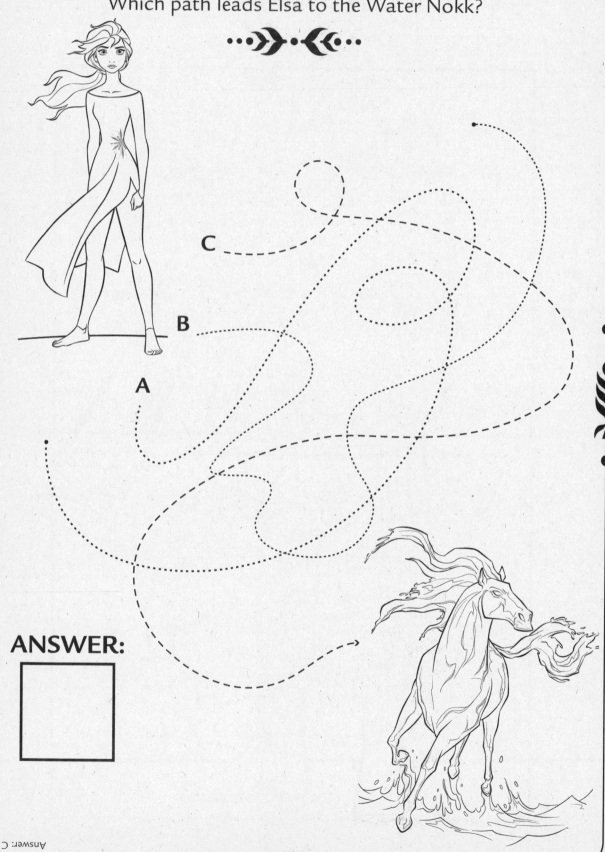

A

B

C

ANSWER:

LET'S DRAW

Use the grid below
to draw Olaf.

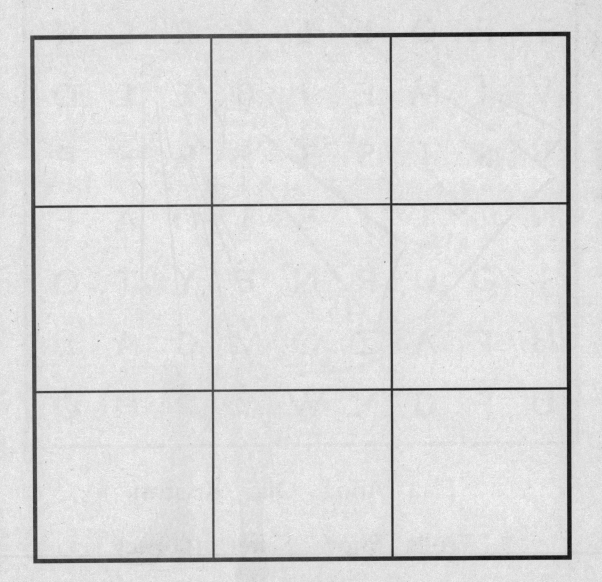

WORD SEARCH

Can you find the words in the grid below?

S D K A N N A X L L

C K W C B O L A F

T R O L L S R E K

V I M E J B E L D

F S I S T E R S P

N T I J S I O A F

J O U R N E Y T O

H F A Z O M G A L

U F G N W Y P H Q

Elsa Anna Olaf Kristoff

Trolls Snow Sister Journey

MISSING PIECE

Can you find the missing piece of the puzzle?

A

B

C

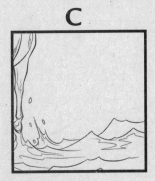

WORD UNSCRAMBLE

Unscramble the words below.

SENV

_____

NAAN

_____

SELA

_____

LFOA

_____

© Disney

BUILD-A-WORD

How many words can you make using the letters in:

MAGICAL JOURNEY

EXAMPLE: Crayon

_____   _____

_____   _____

_____   _____

_____   _____

_____   _____

_____   _____

                             _____

                             _____

                             _____

SQUARES

Taking turns, connect a line from one star to another. If you draw a line that completes a square, write your initial in the square. The person with the most squares at the end of the game wins!

TIC-TAC-TOE

Ryder is ready for a challenge!

LET'S DRAW
Use the grid below to draw Olaf.

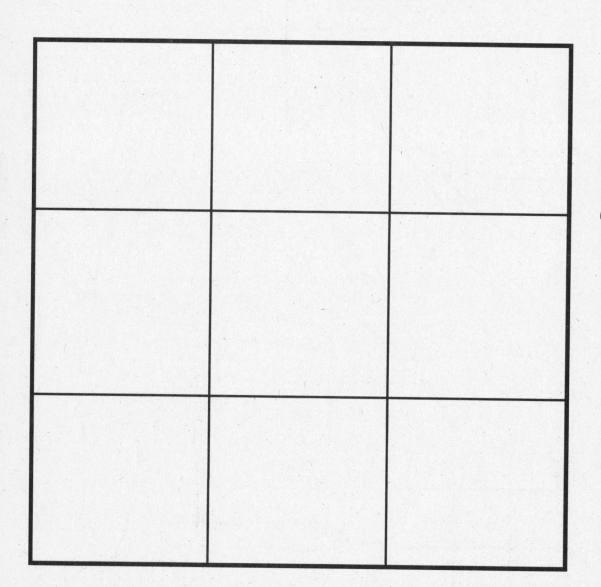

MISSING PIECE

Can you find the missing piece of the puzzle?

A

B

C

HOW MANY?

How many pictures of Anna do you see?

ANSWER:

MATCHING
Which shadow is the correct match?

A

B

ANSWER:

© Disney

SPOT THE DIFFERENCE

Find the 3 differences between the two pictures.

A

B

© Disney

© Disney

TIC-TAC-TOE

Mattias is ready for a challenge!

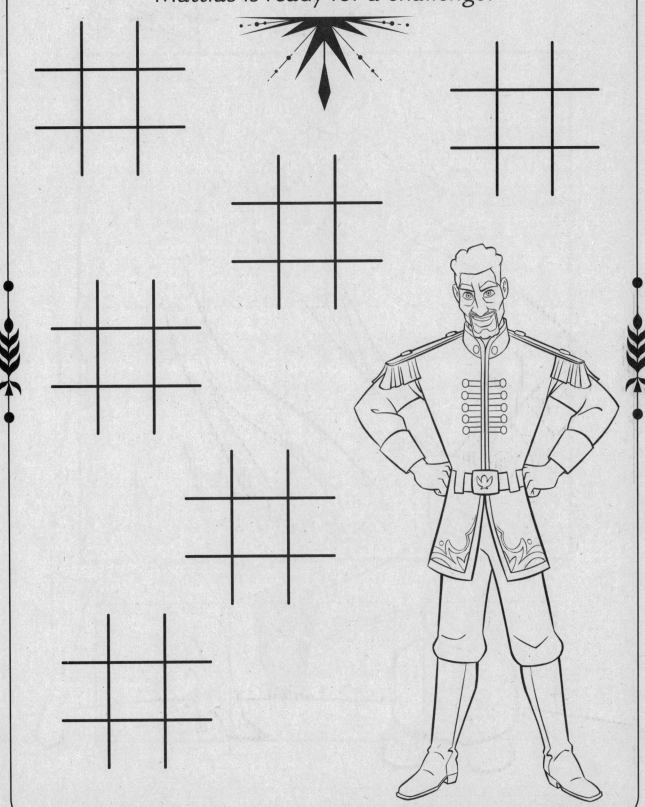

MISSING PIECE

Can you find the missing piece of the puzzle?

A

B

C

A-MAZE-ING

Lead Elsa through the maze to find Anna.

START

FINISH

HOW MANY?

How many pictures of Elsa do you see?

ANSWER:

CRACK THE CODE

Using the secret code below, fill in the blanks
to reveal the hidden message!

● ● ● ● ● ●

A	B	C	D	E	F	G	H	I	J	K	L	M
1	2	3	4	5	6	7	8	9	10	11	12	13
N	O	P	Q	R	S	T	U	V	W	X	Y	Z
14	15	16	17	18	19	20	21	22	23	24	25	26

___ ___ ___ ___ ___ ___ ___ ___
19 20   5 16 16   9 14   7

___ ___ ___ ___
 9 14 20 15

___ ___ ___
20   8   5

___ ___ ___ ___ ___ ___ ___
21 14 11 14 15 23 14

© Disney

WHICH PATH?

Which path leads Olaf to Anna?

A   B   C

ANSWER:

SPOT THE DIFFERENCE
Find the 3 differences between the two pictures.

A

B

MATCHING

Which shadow is the correct match?

B

A

ANSWER:

Answer: A

A-MAZE-ING

Lead Ryder through the maze to find Honeymaren.

START

FINISH

HOW MANY?

How many pictures of the Fire Spirit do you see?

ANSWER:

Answer: 7

MATCHING

Which shadow is the correct match?

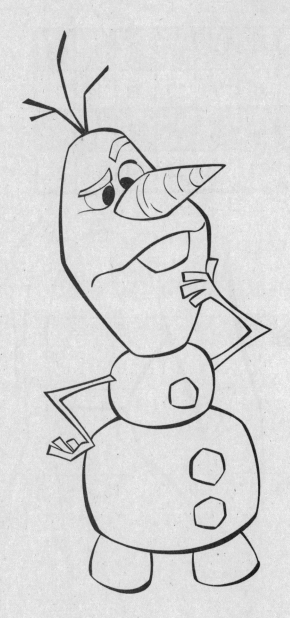

A

B

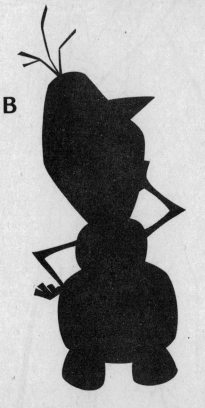

ANSWER:

CRACK THE CODE

Using the secret code below, fill in the blanks to reveal the hidden message!

• • • • • •

A	B	C	D	E	F	G	H	I	J	K	L	M
1	2	3	4	5	6	7	8	9	10	11	12	13
N	O	P	Q	R	S	T	U	V	W	X	Y	Z
14	15	16	17	18	19	20	21	22	23	24	25	26

___ ___ ___ ___ ___
9   7   18   5   23

___ ___   ___ ___
21   16   9   14

___ ___ ___ ___ ___ ___
14   1   20   21   18   5

SPOT THE DIFFERENCE

Find the 3 differences between the two pictures.

A

B

FOLLOW THE PATH

Follow the letters in SVEN in order to find
the correct path through the maze.

START

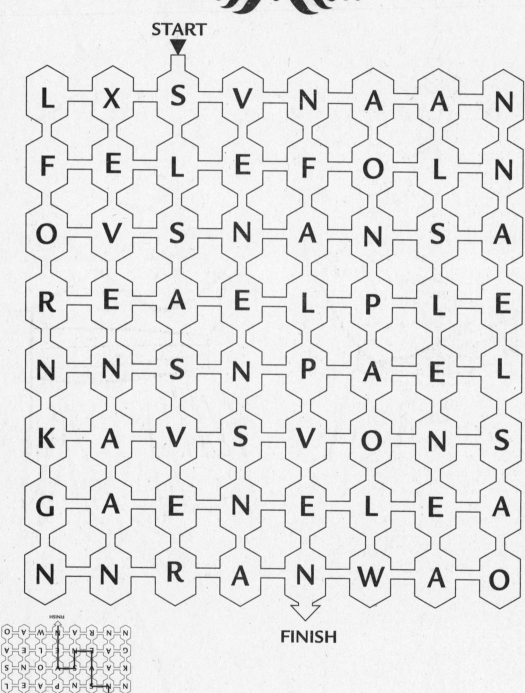

L	X	S	V	N	A	A	N
F	E	L	E	F	O	L	N
O	V	S	N	A	N	S	A
R	E	A	E	L	P	L	E
N	N	S	N	P	A	E	L
K	A	V	S	V	O	N	S
G	A	E	N	E	L	E	A
N	N	R	A	N	W	A	O

FINISH

© Disney

WHICH PATH?

Which path leads Elsa to Olaf?

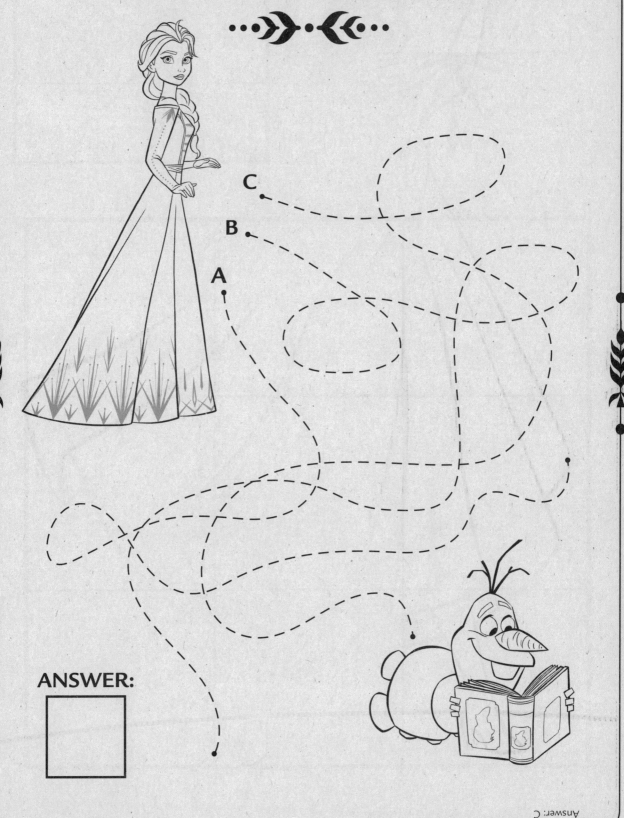

C

B

A

ANSWER:

LET'S DRAW

Use the grid below
to draw Sven.

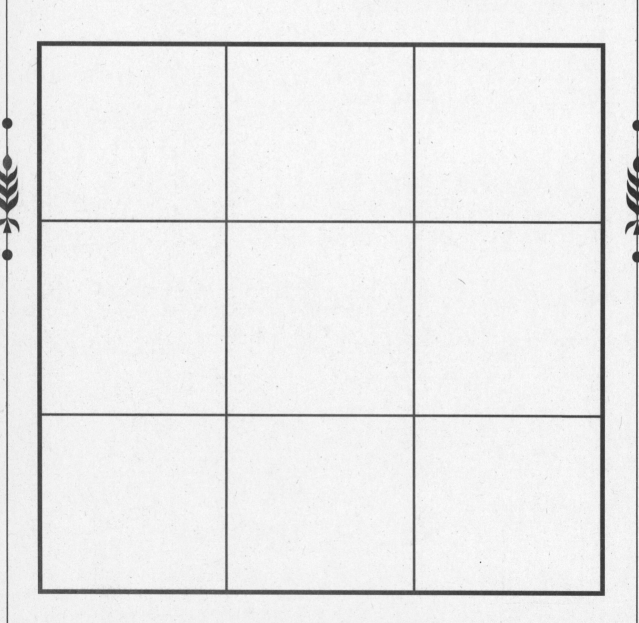